MYTHS AND LEGENDS OF THE MOUNTAINS

MYTHS AND LEGENDS OF THE MOUNTAINS

Myths and Legends Come in all Forms, Be it Man or Animal

FOUR SHORT STORIES

HARRY EVERLY

Harry Everly Story Collections
Colorado Springs, CO

Myths and Legends of the Mountains: Myths and Legend Come in All Forms, Be It Man or Animal

Copyright © 2019 by Harry Everly

Inquiries may be made to the author at:
harmancolorado@gmail.com

Independantly published by Harry Everly.

Cover Design: Valerie Rivera-Dyer of StylePoint Design

Interior Design: Robert Dyer of StylePoint Design

Edited by: Robert Dyer of StylePoint Design

www.stylepointdesign.com

ISBN-13: 978-1-7979-7396-8
ISBN-10: 1-7979-7396-7

Printed in U.S.A.

DEDICATION

In loving memory, to my wife Jo, who I miss very much. She was always there to carry my extra camera gear while I was out front trying to get that next beautiful picture, all the while I just needed to turn around.

To all those who encouraged and supported me especially my sister Sharon and brother Bob. And to our dog, Cactus, who watched me night after night not knowing for sure what I was doing but keeping me company.

Table of Contents

Night of the Wolves

Preface

The Grey Wolf, (Canis Lupus), was sometimes called the Timber Wolf, the Western Wolf, and even the Mexican Wolf. Depending on the part of the country you come from. This true canine native at one time inhabited the early wilderness and remote areas of Mexico, Northwest America, and Canada.

Once they had great numbers, but man hunted them to protect their livestock or just for sport to collect bounty on their hides. Significantly their numbers began to drop to dangerous levels.

Wolves live in groups called packs, with a leader called an alpha male along with his mate, an alpha female. They say it's very rare for wolves to kill humans as they often live far from human contact. Most wolves developed a natural fear of man.

With all things in nature, things have a way of correcting according to circumstances. Nature always seems to find a way to reset itself.

This is the story of one pack of wolves trying to survive in the land we call Yellowstone, within a great valley called Lamar Valley. The Lamar River runs through it and it's often called the American Serengeti, named so for the many different species of wildlife living in this area. The Lamar Valley is home to a large pack of Western Grey Wolves. The year was 1827 and this is where our story begins.

Chapter 1
Blue Eyes

The pack was closing in on a lone elk. Chances of the elk escaping were getting dimmer with each second that went by. The alpha male was leading the hunt, and he had the pack moving as one unit. The huge elk was trapped but stood his ground. To get the elk's attention, the alpha did as he always did, and struck first. Then three others from the pack attacked. Two jumped on his back. A third went for the rear leg. A tactic used many times before. The big elk turned as soon as he felt the wolves on his back. That was all the alpha needed as he went for the throat. Vise like jaws crushed the windpipe, and before long it was all over.

This was the first real good meal the pack had in a long time. The long cold brutal winter hampered their hunting. Most of the big game left the area for better conditions. Each member of the pack got a share according to their ranking. This meal was the first for a long time, but it wasn't nearly enough.

The alpha was called Blue Eyes, this due to his deep blue piercing eyes. The name all mountain men in this area knew. He was somewhat larger and much smarter than the other members of his pack. His alpha mate was a smaller female. All mountain men and hunters who knew this pack, named her Miss. Other male pack members knew Miss was Blue Eyes' and off limits. Miss was never that far from Blue Eyes when he was around. Together they had many litters of pups, providing care for each and every pup till they grew up and moved out of the pack. The pack also took extra good care of each litter. They knew Blue Eyes and Miss were their meal ticket.

Hunting mostly after nightfall, the mountain men began to call them the night pack. They were a large pack of about twenty full grown wolves and between six to eight pups. They needed to hunt if they were going to survive. There was just too many of them, way too many mouths that were always hungry. They would hunt everything from buffalo, deer, elk, and time to time a young or wounded bear. The pack was starving and now went after anything to satisfy their hunger. This made them very dangerous. If they were going to survive Blue Eyes would have to push them to hunt. Hunger and weakness were not an option.

Blue Eyes was a very intelligent and a fast learner. He knew when man set traps baited with poison, ensuring each member of his pack would stay away. He would keep the pack at a safe distance from man so none would be shot by hunters.

Why, he would even sneak at night into the campsites of men, managing to steal their food to bring it back to the pups. He was a great leader and provider, but hunger was beginning to be a major problem. This put extra pressure on Blue Eyes to keep the pack fed as game was getting harder and harder to find. Even man would not be safe.

Chapter 2
Human Kill

The Rocky Mountain Fur Company sent out two members of their party to hunt for food. Using all their hunting skills, by late afternoon, they were able to jump and shoot a huge buck.

Blue Eyes' sharp ears picked up the sound of the gun fire from far off. This, to him, meant food. It would be there for the taking for the pack. It was time to gather up his hunting pack which included all except two older females, who stayed behind to care and protect the pups. Anticipating the coming hunt, and with great excitement, off the pack went with Blue Eyes and Miss leading them out.

His pack arrived just before sunset and getting close enough to see the hunters skinning the deer and cutting up sections of meat to pack back to camp. Very soon, they would be heading off to join the others of their company, providing a warm meal of meat. Blue Eyes and his pack had different plans.

Working ever closer Blue Eyes waited till the time was right before setting their plan into action. The pack knew what was required of them and moved out on Blue Eyes' signal to surround the hunters. Again, Blue Eyes was the first to spring the attack.

The two hunters were caught by surprise as they were busy packing the meat for the journey back to their camp. The hunters never had a chance to get their guns out as it happened so quickly. The pack was able to kill both hunters and three horses. This now made them more than animals. It made them killers and now they had their first human kills.

The pack fed on everything as quickly as they could. Blue Eyes sensed they needed to leave the area. Not much was left but a few members took some meat back for the pups and their keepers. Miss would lead them back into the forest toward their den. All that is, except Blue Eyes. He would stay behind to guard their retreat which he did after every kill to ensure they weren't being followed.

Chapter 3
The Retreat

Blue Eyes was still there hiding in the brush early the next morning when the rest of the fur company came across the slaughter. All of the men were in shock, as they couldn't believe their eyes. Two Indian scouts informed the company leader they recognized the footprints of wolves and they were the culprits. Digging one big hole they buried what little there was left. The leader of the fur company spoke some last words over them before he set his Indian scouts out to follow the tracks.

Watching from the brush, this was Blue Eyes' cue to lead them away. They followed for some distance what seemed to be good, deep tracks laid down by Blue Eyes. This was Blue Eyes' plan, as all night he had laid down readable tracks to a stream near some rocks. Blue Eyes was hoping they would take his bait. Yea! He was real smart. He had also taught Miss to lead the pack back to the den using a different trail. This meant going about a mile out of their way crossing rocks when they could.

The scouts took the bait. They lost the tracks a short time later, when they reached rocks by the stream. Leading them away with his tracks ensured, the scouts couldn't follow the rest of the pack back to the den. Frustrated and confused both Indian scouts seemed to give up. Blue Eyes was very smart having them track him. He hid again, watching them till they rode back to the fur company camp site. Blue Eyes followed, out of sight and behind, making sure they had given up before joining his pack back at the den.

The pack got a meal but not much for so many. It wouldn't be long before all would need more. Miss was waiting and glad to see Blue Eyes when he got back safely. It was now time to rest and digest his meal before another hunt. For a short time, Blue Eyes stood watch to ensure he wasn't followed. Miss snuggled in close beside him. Then, being assured he wasn't followed, Blue Eyes closed his eyes for a well-deserved rest.

Chapter 4
Losing Miss

The sun was beginning to set when the pack became restless. Blue Eyes knew the pack was hungry and it was time to hunt again. As always, the pups and a couple of older females stayed behind. The hunting pack went off led by Blue Eyes and Miss.

He led them to the top of a ridge looking down for game. His keen sense of smell picked up smoke. The pack reacted to his gesture and stayed put as he went high on a boulder to look out across the valley below.

There, about a mile below him, he spotted a campfire in the distance, the same direction as the smoke. He knew it to be human. The pack followed when Blue Eyes led them closer. Within site of the camp, the pack instinctively spread out surrounding the camp, but staying put 'till Blue Eyes was ready. Blue Eyes looked into the camp. Like any good general of his army he evaluated the camp. He could see a man sleeping near the fire. Another man at the fire was standing guard with a gun, and still another was checking on the horses. The guard with the gun would be his target.

Keeping low, Blue Eyes began to move in. The rest of the huge pack moved in slowly. They were just waiting for Blue Eyes to make his move. Suddenly the horses were spooked. One member of the pack got close enough that they picked up the wolf's scent. The guard by the fire became alert spotting Miss coming from the brush. Quickly he got a shoot off toward Miss before Blue Eyes could pounce. Chaos broke out as all the wolves attacked man and horses alike.

Again, the attack provided a meal but at a cost. The guard was able to put a slug into Miss. Blue Eyes went to her. Trying in vain to get her up but she was gone. A deep rage came over him, and he took it out on the one member of the pack who spooked the horses. He did this to show his dominance.

The pack took out their rage also on the downed horses, tearing them to shreds along with the dead bodies of three humans. They ate their fill, leaving a slaughter that would be difficult to behold. Blue Eyes stayed just long enough to sit and have one long last look at his beloved Miss. Head down, off he went. He led the pack back to the den to feed the pups and the remaining wolves. That night you could hear his howl for miles, feeling the lost within his heart for his beloved Miss.

Chapter 5
The Trap

It wasn't the wildlife in the area Blue Eyes wanted now. It was the humans that dared to enter his territory. He left the cave, while the others were resting. He scouted for humans. He wanted vengeance to ease his broken heart. A few miles from the den he spotted what was remained of the Rocky Mountain Fur Company. He followed them 'till they stopped to make camp. Shortly afterwards he hurried back to the den. He had found what he was looking for. Tonight's raid would be the vengeance he wanted so badly. He was not now thinking as a leader, but as a wolf filled with rage. But Blue Eyes didn't realized that as he was watching, he too was being watched. The leader of the pack was not playing it safe anymore.

The fur company earlier that day came across last night's raid and slaughter. The leader of the fur company had his scouts circle wide around the remaining group as they traveled. One scout was lucky enough to spot Blue Eyes coming up on the group. He watched the big wolf leave when they came upon the camp and went to inform the leader of what he saw. The leader knew this lone wolf was following them for a reason. He believed now that the lone wolf was from the killer pack. If this was so, then the killer wolf pack would spring their surprise attack later that night. It was time for the fur company leader to prepare a little surprise trap of his own.

The men placed grass, dirt and sticks under some blankets, trying to make it seem they were sleeping around the fire. Two men volunteered to keep the fire going posing as guards. They tethered all the horse close to camp. Then a few men climbed some trees and positioned themselves to see down into the camp around the fire. Others dug deep holes to bury themselves. Having other men cover them up with a blanket with dirt and brush. They left just enough room to see and extend out their guns. Others position themselves partly in the river with their guns trained on the only direction the wolves could come from. The trap was now ready, and the leader sat and waited with the two guards. His loaded flint pistols were lying next to his side, cocked and ready. Now all just had to wait as night began to close in.

Chapter 6
The Pack's Demise

Blue Eyes led his hunting pack from the den for the first time without Miss, leaving the pups and two caretakers behind. His rage now was affecting his caution. He headed at great speed straight to the human camp, not realizing he only had but one pathway in. This meant he couldn't surround the camp as he had done before. He had but only one option. It meant they had to rush straight in. In the past, he would have walked away from this with his pack. He wouldn't have given up such a huge advantage of surrounding his prey. His rage dulled his thinking.

He only wanted the humans killed. The pack waited, knowing there was going to be a rush into the camp led by Blue Eyes. They didn't have to wait long. A slow walk at first, then, the pace picked up when Blue Eyes saw the man-leader turning in his direction. All hell erupted as fire came from above and from men jumping from cover.

Blue Eyes leaped at the leader but felt the sting of his pistol shot. Falling off to the side he watched his pack getting wiped out before his eyes. The shot had hit him in the spine, and he could hardly move. His back legs had no feeling.

Within five minutes it was over. Blue Eyes hunting pack was dead or dying. The men were putting wolves out of their pain with a bullet to the head, all that is, except Blue Eyes. He tried to get up and attack the leader when he approached. He had no control of his hind legs. His anger still raged within, as the leader of the fur company approached him. He tried to drag himself toward the leader, but he stopped. The leader looked down on him, pointed his pistol at his head and fired. Blue Eyes and the night pack were all at peace. The leader of the Rocky Mountain Fur Company was sure this was the wolf pack that had killed so many.

They burned all the bodies of the wolves, and they felt sad that it had all came down to this. Some in the company wanted to save the hides to sell. The leader saw how thin the wolves were and knew they only attacked because of hunger. Yes, we knew that to be true at the beginning, but are we sure that was the real reason at the end?

Epilogue

What ever happened to the pups and caretakers back at the den when the pack never returned? It seemed another lone male wolf came around shortly afterwards. He took them to join his pack and provided food, moving them to a better feeding area where his pack began to grow.

Isn't it kind of ironic? With nature, all things just seems to have a way of working out. Just days after Blue Eyes and his hunting pack were wiped out, along comes another male wolf, saving the remaining pack members. Coincidence?

Perhaps not!

You see that lone wolf was one of the sons of Blue Eyes and Miss. As with all in nature, the cycle of life continues. Family and nature wins out again in the end.

Monarch of the Pass

Preface

For many years I've been going with my wife to Estes Park, Colorado to visit the Rocky Mountain National Park, visiting mostly in the fall when the wild elk take over the town. We see them everywhere, in neighborhoods, in the streets of town and even on the golf course.

People come from miles, all parts of the country and far away to view this annual spectacle. This time of year, all get to witness the big bulls gathering the female cows, for it is now the time of the rutting season. The quietness being broken by Male elk sounding off their loud bugle mating calls for all within ear shot. A large mature male bull with a grand antler rack is often called a monarch who displays a posture of one who reigns supreme.

I often wondered, could it be, the Native American Indians would have their own stories of these magnificent animals. I really hoped they did.

If not, my imagination took over and I wrote this short story you are about to read. It's a fictional story about a legend born high in the Rockies even before the mountain man came west. No, this was not about an original legend about a brave Indian or even the mighty grizzly bear. It's about the life of one rather huge mighty elk growing up and becoming a monarch. Please sit back and enjoy my story, *Monarch of the Pass*.

Chapter 1
Monarch's Loss

The life of this young elk started out like any other baby elk calf. Having a mother who cared and protected him from harm. This would be her last calf for she was getting along in years. He was about a year old when this monarch's legend began.

Indian braves were out hunting when they came upon our young elk for the first time. A true young monarch of an elk no doubt about it; giving him the name of Monarch from that day forward. What made this elk special? It was there for all to see. He was much taller and packed with muscle. He loved to run, and he ran very fast, sure he could. He leaped, and what a leaper, better than 15 yards at full speed and with ease. His hearing and vision was extra sharp. He could smell a bear coming a half mile away, sighting trouble from afar, always ensuring his mother was well out of danger and safe at a long distance. When the Indian hunting party did spot him, he would prance off as soon as they began to follow. Monarch would let them close in, and then, like a flash of lighting, off he went leaving them far behind. As for the trailing Indian hunting party, they never got close enough to test their skills.

Monarch always left his mother in the forest as he went to check out the meadows and streams. He always did this before bringing her down to graze and drink. One cool fall day Monarch left his mother in the forest while inspecting the area, ensuring it was safe. All seemed quite so he drank from the stream before heading back to fetch his mother.

A young brave, out to prove himself a man, and hunting on his own and on his feet, came upon Monarch's mother in the trees. Spying the cow, he slowly made his way close, being as quiet as he could be. He was upwind of her. Monarch's mother didn't hear him or pick up his scent. He loaded an arrow, drew back his bow, took careful aim, then released an arrow into her heart. She took two steps and dropped just as Monarch was returning to get her.

Hearing the zing of the arrow, Monarch stopped, and looking he now spotting the young brave. Monarch's first instinct was to charge the brave, but there was much distance between them. Monarch instinctively knew the young brave would have enough time to draw another arrow and shoot before he got there. He turned away, and after one last look at his dead mother, ran and leaped from there as quick as he could.

Monarch ran for miles, getting higher up into the mountain pass before hiding behind an outcrop of large boulders. Now it was beginning to sink in what had just happen. Feeling the sense of loss Monarch was missing his mother. There was nothing more Monarch could have done, and his survival was all he thought of. A long cold lonely night without his mother was something Monarch hadn't experienced. He was now all alone. Tomorrow would be a new chapter in his life.

Chapter 2
Young Prime Bull

Three years had passed, and Monarch roamed the high mountain pass. This outcrop of boulders was now his summer sanctuary away from the outside world, only leaving for trips down below to spend fall rut and winters in the warmer valleys.

He always returned to his mountain domain in the late spring.

Our young Monarch was now reaching his prime. He was now beginning to feel the urge bucks feel in the fall. Mating season was in full swing and he was looking for mating cows of his own. Some will say Monarch is why many bulls gather their cows together. The other bulls bugle call was an alarm to let other bucks know Monarch was in the area. Whether it was a warning call or mating call, you can be the judge of that. Other male elks preferred to have nothing to do with Monarch, running away when he approached. He would fill his need and obligation then head back high into the pass tired but insuring a new generation of calf's come spring.

During another fall rut a rather large bull decided he wanted to challenge Monarch for the right to mate the cows. This was a wrong move on his part. The ensuing battle lasted nearly five minutes. Monarch put him to shame without hardly a scratch to himself. There were no more challenges from that point on.

Witnessing this battle for the rights, our young brave, now a warrior, watched them from a distance. Killing an elk bull for himself already, dressing it out, the warrior would leave Monarch in peace. Believing there would be another time and place for their encounter. Monarch had no idea this was the young brave who killed his mother years before.

Monarch kept a close eye on our young brave. He watched as he packed all the meat on a pack horse, watching him mount his horse and seeing both horses head off. Again, it was time for Monarch to give his full attention back to his females. Another rutting season had come and gone.

Two more years of rutting seasons passed. Then one season, returning to the mountain pass, Monarch came surprisingly upon a grizzly bear. Our warrior, out scouting for intruders, was also a witness to this encounter. He sat astride his horse watched from a distance this ongoing battle between Monarch and the grizzly. Monarch's strength and magnificent rack was more than a match for the huge bear. The warrior couldn't believe his eyes as Monarch pick the bear up with his antlers, slammed the bear down and speared him dead. Then Monarch turned his head, looking toward the brave sitting astride his horse, as if he knew he was there all the time. Monarch shook his antlers and pranced away into the woods knowing the brave would never get close enough for a kill.

Monarch's blood line was secure as he had sired many a calf. Monarch lived within that pass for many years. Monarch knew the pass well, and never traveled the same path twice in a row. He was a true loner in his land. Monarch wanted it that way. He was the ruler of this pass up in the mountain.

Chapter 3
One Last Hunt

Years passed and Monarch was older now, and in the later years of his life. Monarch still was a sight to behold. He has maybe two or three more seasons if he was lucky. The brave warrior who shot his mother had seen him many times over the years. One night while sitting in his teepee thinking about all the years he hunted in vain, it came to him. He believed he now knew how to hunt him down. He remembered how he got close to Monarch's mother while on foot. He was willing to test it, knowing the time was running out for one last hunt for such a fine trophy. He hoped hunting on foot would work again. He spent four days roaming the mountain pass, but his luck seemed hopeless. He would soon need to head back to his village. The village knowing of his failure was something he would have to live with. Maybe in his mind the Great Spirit wanted it so. Being tired, he laid down beside a tree, and fell asleep. For now, going back would wait.

He awoke to the sound of something coming through the brush directly right in front of him. He remained still, only pulling his bow up preparing to shoot hoping it wasn't a bear. There, walking out from the brush was Monarch. His chance had come. He pulled the arrow back. Then something happened that puzzled him. Monarch looked him straight in the eyes. Monarch made no attempt to run excepting the fate which was coming. They eyed each other before the warrior slowly lowered his bow and showed his respect to Monarch with a nod of his head. Monarch proudly raised his head high turned and walk back into the brush. Was the Indian warrior overcome by something only the Great Spirit knew? He watched Monarch until he vanished from sight, and then he stood up, slowly walking back to his village. Along the way he was glad he had not killed this magnificent animal.

Riding the mountain pass from time to time, he would spot Monarch from a distance. He always acknowledged him with a nod of respect before letting Monarch go in peace. Believing from that day on all would proclaim this elk the Monarch of the Pass.

Epilogue

Two years later the brave spotted him for the last time. They both looked at each other. Only this time, after the brave nodded his respect, Monarch lowered and raised his head in return. Then turned and moved on. Monarch was never seen again.

When the mountain men arrived on the mountain, they inquired about the mountain pass. The young brave who became a warrior was now a chief. The chief looked to the pass proclaiming it, from that time on, Monarch Pass. Having them sit as he told the story of how Monarch's spirit runs through this mountain pass, a great Indian legend born for all time.

Roar in the Mountain

Preface

They called him Mountain Tom, six-foot three, tough as nails, mountain man. He'd been trapping the High Sierra Nevada Mountains and going north toward Oregon from California for the last seven years. He was respected by the Indians but civilization he wanted very little to do with, unless he wanted to trade his pelts for supplies. Riding his old horse, his companion he called Paint, they traveled every mile of the mountains he loved. He had seen about everything one could ever see. The story of his encounter with a myth or legend would scare even a seasoned mountain man like Tom. It was a fear that raced through him when he heard the roar in the mountain.

Chapter 1
The Roar

It was early July in the year 1850. Riding his Paint deep in the mountains near a valley the Indians called Yosemite. He enjoyed the magnificent views and he never got tired of them. Some ten miles on, he and Paint stopped for a refreshing drink from a cold mountain stream. Tom rested. Paint was mowing down the rich grass beside the stream when he heard a roar off in the distance that made both him and Paint jump. It was a roar so loud that it raised every hair on the back of his neck, maybe even Paint's.

His first reaction was to grab the Hawkins rifle and search for a big boulder to hide behind, while securing the reins of his horse so it wouldn't run off. There was one last roar even further off in the distance before he and Paint began to settle down—a mighty roar, scaring years off his life, that he had never heard before. Until now he only heard about these roars through the Indian's stories while visiting their village. He believed them to be tall tales—until now. He thought about it and came to believe the roar was so loud due to the sound bouncing off the high mountain walls. Well, that explanation sounded good to him, he reckoned. His next decision was either to follow or take the smart way out and go in the opposite direction. His curiosity got the better of him. Although Paint had an all-out different view.

"Paint old boy I know you rather go a different way but believe me it's a bear and I could use some good steaks. Besides, his hide would bring us some much-needed supplies." he said as he mounted up.

There was one last refusal by Paint but to no avail. Tom jerked the reins and kicked his flank and off they went riding, off toward the sound.

Chapter 2
Help Coming

It was approximately an hour later when Tom and Paint came across what looked like a kill. It was a big elk, but something was not right. The elk was dead alright, but there was no sign of a wound only a broken neck. It hadn't been dead long as no scavengers had feasted on the carcass. All of a sudden, a roar, much louder this time, scared a few years off of Tom's life. This time the mountains were not the reason for the loud roar. Maybe Paint's idea of going the other direction wasn't so bad. Again, the Hawkins gun was put to the ready as he scanned the area for any movement.

Out of the corner of his eye he spotted two Indian scouts coming into view from the forest. He raised his rifle to show he met no harm as they in turn raised their bows and rode on in. As they got closer, he recognized them as the Nisenan from the local Maidu tribe; a local tribe he had a very good friendship with, and he knew the two braves. One brave, Running Elk, was the son of the Chief, Two Moons, and the other was his good friend, Little Fox.

"Running Elk and Little Fox, good to see you."

"Tom, you heard the sound of Tall Man?" said Running Elk.

"I don't believe in Tall Man. I think it was a bear."

"No bear kills elk without leaving marks or bites." said Running Elk.

"Maybe the elk fell and broke its neck running away from it." said Tom.

"Tom, you heard the roar, not roar of bear."

"Yes, no bear roar I've ever heard before, but no man could roar that loud."

"Not man, Bigfoot, who walks like man on two feet, for I have seen his big tracks." said Little Fox.

"A myth, for he has never been seen and I've seen many bears walk on two feet."

"Come, such nonsense. Help me skin this elk and we'll have fresh meat tonight." said Tom.

A little later, a warm fire and fresh meat filled their bellies before they settled down to sleep.

Suddenly—a scream—just a short distance from their camp, startled each man. They heard something run away, and it was nearby. More wood was placed on the fire to light up the area and they took turns standing guard the rest of the night. Sleep was delayed and it would wait. One last loud roar far off into the night filled their ears.

Chapter 3
The Tracking Begins

The morning sun felt warm as they began to move around. It wasn't long before Little Fox called the others to his location. When they arrived he pointed down to rather some large tracks; tracks that were not of a bear but somewhat of a very large creature. Running Elk looked at Tom.

"There, see? Tall Man was here."

He placed his hand into the track.

Whatever it was, it was only about twenty five yards from their camp. Why would he scream so close to their camp? It wasn't long before they discovered the reason. He must have stepped over a log on top of a rattlesnake which bit him before he ripped it apart and ran away.

"We should track him, maybe the snake bite will slow him down some." said Tom.

"The three of us should." said Running Elk.

About that time, they heard the roar again some distance away. Quickly they gathered their belongings and mounted their horses, riding off in the direction of the sound. The only smart one was Paint who thought the other way was still the best.

Little Fox led the way due to his tracking ability. Each time they thought they lost his trail a loud roar put them back on track. Tom realized, whatever it was, it wanted them to follow. If Tom was by himself, maybe he would have taken Paint's advice, and he would have headed in the other direction.

Two days had come and gone. At times Tom had that uneasy feeling they were being watched when they made camp for the evening. Early the next day, again that feeling came upon Tom when they topped a hill. There, in a distance, he spotted something.

Chapter 4
Terror

He wasn't sure but it seemed to have been upright and tall, the likes he had never seen before. It quickly ducked behind some thick brush. Tom was sure it was watching them. Wanting them to see it. Running Elk thought he saw the same thing. Whatever it could have been it was surely taking them further out of their familiar area. Running Elk and Little Fox mentioned it would be a good idea if one of them would circle wide getting ahead of it. Tom was not fond of the idea and couldn't convince them it was a bad decision. Little Fox rode off but wasn't aware he had been spotted. Now he was the one was being targeted.

Running Elk and Tom approached the location slowly. They went in the direction in which they both thought they saw the creature hiding. Sure enough, they could tell something had been there. What they saw next put a chill in their spine—tracks heading straight off in the direction Little Fox was circling. Both men knew it was time to throw caution to the wind. Little Fox was in extreme danger. They determined where they thought Little Fox would be heading and wasted no time getting there.

Chapter 5
The Encounter

Over the next two hills they spotted a place they thought Little Fox might be. A weathered rocky hillside with plenty of rocks in which he might be on top viewing. They couldn't see him. Paint didn't want to enter the bottom of the rocky hillside but again he got over ruled. They rode down to the base of the rocks looking for any sign of Little Fox or something more dangerous.

Suddenly a rockslide got their attention, and they were able to ride off to a safe distance just in time. They were sure it was no coincidence that the rocks began to fall. Still there was no sign of Little Fox. They knew that the creature was somewhere on top of the rocky hillside. It surely must have started the rockslide, which only mean it was going down the backside. They rode quickly to get to the top. Sure enough, when they got to the other side, they saw its tracks heading off into the nearby trees. They were close but where was Little Fox? Riding very slowly and following his tracks, off they pursued in the direction of the thick trees, being very aware something was waiting for them—a place it wanted them to be.

An hour's distance into the trees they stopped to get a look over the very dense area. Tom thought maybe it was raining as he felt what seemed to be rain drops. Wiping his neck, he discovered it was blood. Looking up only to see Little Fox impaled through his chest from a broken limb. A roar from deep inside the forest let them know they were in its domain.

They turned their horses at a quick pace heading back out in the way they came. Out in the open they went, away from the forest edge. They felt safe for now. It was late afternoon and they knew the two of them were up against something they were unable to cope with.

Chapter 6
Being Hunted

Running Elk wanted to press on with the hunt, but Tom was beginning to second guess Running Elk's decision. Moving on meant they were down one person and they would have to be even more cautious. They would be in its territory and maybe there could be more. Running Elk finely agreed, deciding it was time to leave the area and this time Paint didn't need a kick to his flank to move out.

Both men rode until nightfall. Rain began to fall before they stopped to let their horses drink from a small stream. All seemed quite as they drank some water before they heard the roar from a distance and knew they were now being hunted. They just had to keep moving late into the night.

Rain was now coming down harder when Running Elk spotted what looked like a cave. It wasn't deep but it kept them out of the rain. Raining this hard, they believed that whatever was following would have to hold up also. A few hours of sleep was needed, and each man took a turn to stand guard. An hour before sunrise the rain had stopped. Tom thought it would be good if they headed out to keep whatever distance they achieved between them and the creature.

The sun rose to another day. Hours later they stopped on top of a hill to scout the trail behind them. Not hearing anything for a while, and not seeing anything either, they decided to keep moving. They got back on their horses, and then as they were leaving, they heard a roar from far off. It was very loud, and it was letting them know it had spotted them. Any thought of it giving up was gone. If they could not get back to the safety of Running Elk's village, they needed some kind of plan. Could they outsmart a worthy opponent?

Chapter 7
The Plan

Pushing their horses hard, they were able to keep the same distance. They were hungry and tired. They could not afford to stop but the horses needed water. They made a quick stop beside a river which Tom knew flowed through a high mountain pass, a pass with a narrow trail atop a deep river gorge. A plan came to Tom as they rode toward the pass. It was time to inform Running Elk of his plan, and he agreed fully. They needed to do something as another roar meant it was gaining.

Tom had a bear trap in his pack. He would set it in the middle of the narrow trail hoping to impair its foot giving them enough time to attack with their weapons. Again, another roar but this time even much closer. Tired horses convinced Running Elk this could be their only hope, but did they have time on their side.

Reaching the high mountain trail, they found a great spot to set their trap. It was a very narrow section that was just wide enough for a man to ride a horse. Tom set the trap ensuring it was covered carefully. Running Elk took the horses some distance further down the trail and out of sight.

Both men climbed up higher off the trail and had a good view looking down with gun and bow ready. They thought separating would give them a better chance to get a clean shot as they heard another close roar coming up the trail.

Staying out of sight they waited. Time passed. It wouldn't be long now before they could see what had been following them. Tom looked at Running Elk who shook his head not seeing anything. Something was not right. A little more time passed then they heard something above them.

Sure enough, it had figured out their plan and circled high above them. Their view of it was very short and they knew it was nothing like they ever saw before. Man, or beast, they had no time to stop and catch a better look but, scrambled down the mountain just ahead of it.

Chapter 8
The Plan Worked

Half running and half tumbling they were able to stay just ahead, finally reaching the trail. Running, and then jumping over the trap they flew. The creature reached the trail following close before he placed its foot directly on to the trigger. The trap closed surrounding its ankle. A scream let both men know it was caught. Turning then to see its mighty strength pull the jaws apart and freeing its foot before throwing the trap down into the river.

This was just enough time for both men to raise their weapons, aim and fire. Another scream echoed through the canyon. Their aim was good. They watched as the creature tumbled down the mountainside and into the river. They did not know for sure what it was they had killed, but they were glad to see it hit the river rapids and float further downstream. Hopefully it was dead.

Not wanting to follow the river in hopes of finding what it was, both men recovered their horses. They took one last long look behind them to ensure nothing was there, before setting off on the hard ride to Running Elks village.

Chapter 9
Myth No More?

Their story was the talk of the village. Chief Two Moons said he had heard of this creature they called Tall Man. He had never seen it but heard its roar many moons ago. Hearing many a story from the other area tribes about this man-beast. A man-beast they sometimes called Sasquatch.

Two days later he stopped to rest letting Paint get a drink. Tom thought about the ordeal he and Running Elk experienced. He was still not sure what it was, but he knew he never wanted to meet up with another one. Mounting Paint, he heard a roar in the not-to-far distance. His fear was confirmed when Paint reacted. Maybe a bear? This time Tom took Paint's advice. Letting Paint walk away in the opposite direction. Heading toward civilization leaving forever the roar in the mountain. All the while a pair of eyes gazed down upon them from the forest.

Epilogue

In North American folklore, many would call him Sasquatch or what some like to call Bigfoot. A very hairy, upright-walking, ape-like being who reportedly dwells in the wilderness of California up to British Columbia. Sasquatch a word meaning "wild man or hairy man." A majority of mainstream scientists have historically discounted its existence as they have never found the whole remains of one. What if, they are wrong?

Legend of True Mountain Men

Preface

After the Lewis and Clark expedition the far West opened up for expansion. The stories coming back from the West, from those who dared to explore, opened the eyes of many back East. The lure was great for one such young man named Brad Johnson.

Brad Johnson was fourteen when the Indians raided his family cabin in eastern Ohio. This was such a difficult time for a young lad to grow up. A few years later, life again would change for Brad. Everything Brad had learned allowed his dream of going west to become reality. The West was something he had only heard about.

Seeing the mountains and becoming a mountain man was something he only dreamed about.

Circumstances put it into action. Now it was time to make that dream come true. All that was needed, was going west to the mountains, and finding someone there to teach him to survive. It was Brad's chance for a new life, but in this search, the real reward was finding a true friend. Fate brought Brad and Jim Beaver together. Their life story made them both legends.

Chapter 1
The Attack

It was a cool early fall day when Brad's father and mother saw a band of Indians riding toward them from over the hill top. Brad's father motion to his wife to go back inside the cabin. She instinctively knew what needed to be done. Getting inside, she told Brad to take his ten-year-old sister, Jenny, up deep into the wooded hillside to their designated hiding place. She helped them out the back window and then boarded it up. Then she hurried to the fireplace mantel and grabbed a riffle for her husband.

Brad rushed his sister up the hillside far enough so as not to be spotted. They hid behind some tall brush and looked back toward the cabin. Brad saw his mother hand his father the riffle. His father again motioned her back into the cabin. Upon reaching the cabin she bolted the door shut and the remaining windows. She secured the other gun and went to the front window.

Brad could see a gun barrel protruding from a hole in the front window. He wished he would have stayed behind to defend the cabin with his mother. Yet, according to the family plan he was placed in charge with the task of protecting his younger sister.

As the band of six warrior's road up, Brad's father greeted them with his hand raised in friendship. Suddenly, Brad's mother let out a scream as one warrior put an arrow deep into her husband's chest. Brad kept his sister's head down preventing her from seeing it. That warrior jumped from his horse and ran over to try to scalp him, but Brad's mother fired her gun and the warrior dropped dead before he had the chance. The five remaining warriors broke into the house before she could reload. Hearing his mother's screams, Brad knew it was time for he and his sister to leave.

Pulling his sister along they finally reached another far hill. They looked back to see their cabin burning and the Indians riding away with their horses over the opposite hill. Safe now, Brad let Jenny rest. He took a moment to get his bearings to the neighbor's cabin. Brad estimated about three miles over the next rise. It was all Bard could do to keep Jenny moving as they pressed forward to the Smith's cabin.

They reached the cabin at sunset and informed Morgan Smith and his wife Molly about the attack. The

Smith's assured Brad and his sister that things would be alright and safe in their new cabin home. Brad told Morgan the warriors went off in a different direction. Brad and his sister went along with Mrs. Morgan into the cabin to get some food and rest. Molly comforted the children 'till they fell asleep. Morgan stood watch all night with his gun across his lap.

The next day Morgan and Brad rode to what was left of the Johnson cabin. There wasn't much left standing as it was still smoldering after the fire. They were able to find Brad's parents. Morgan buried them together near a big oak tree. This big tree had fond memories as it was where all of them would gather for picnics when the Morgan's came over to visit. Morgan and Brad rummaged through whatever they could find, and one thing they found included the old gun belonging to Brad's father. There was one last visit to Brad's parent's gravesite before both returned to the Smith's cabin. Brad's sister was waiting. Brad assured Jenny their parents were in a far better place and someday they too would join them. Both now had a new home, new parents and here they could live and be safe.

Chapter 2
Brad Now All Alone

It had been over a year and a half since the attack. Brad was growing up fast under Morgan's tutoring. Almost a man, big for his age and smart beyond his years. It was early spring when Morgan presented Brad the old gun his father had, which he repaired. Morgan taught Brad how to load and use it. Morgan was proud of his new adopted son, if not by name. Jenny was also being a great help for Molly. Morgan made him a coonskin cap for Brad's sixteenth birthday after Brad became fond of Morgan's tales of stories of mountain men and the mountains out West. He wore the hat with pride when he went out hunting.

Brad learned how to track from Morgan and a friendly Indian who knew the family. The Indian taught Brad how to track game and even at times would have Brad track Morgan to perfect his skills. The men in the area said Brad could track better than any Indian and, of course, out shoot any man around. Maybe it was all the mountain men stories that drove him to be the best. Hoping someday to go west and live the mountain life.

Both Brad and Jenny loved their new parents and enjoyed living with them. Every so often they traveled back to the old cabin to visit their parent's graves, pulling weeds and leaving flowers along with a prayer. Life was about as good as it gets, at least for now.

Brad was going on eighteen when he was out tracking wild game on foot one morning. He had just shot a buck and was heading back with some meat when he noticed smoke rising in the direction of the cabin. He dropped the meat and began running as fast as he could. Getting closer, and looking through the trees, he saw the cabin burning.

He saw a body lying near the cabin door. It was Morgan, dead and scalped. Panic set in as he now looked inside the burning cabin for Molly and his sister. He found them but wished he had not. Dead and scalped. Falling to his knees he cried with a pain in his heart he had not felt since the attack on his parents. All the while he wondered why this could be happening to him and he was spared. Personal death again had stepped into his life.

Finding himself all alone he buried the Smith's near their burnt-out cabin. He collected what he could, carrying it with his sister back to his parent's grave. There he laid her to rest alongside his parents. Spending the night, he realized this would be the last time they all would be together before going on his own. Next morning, he set out, realizing there was nothing left there for him. Remembering the stories about the great mountains and the men who became legends out West, he wanted to see and live it for himself.

Early the next morning Brad said a prayer, before one last goodbye for the last time. All alone, he walked out with his father's gun and the little possessions and grub that he could carry. A short distance away he looked back remembering the family he had to leave behind. He now set his sights West, looking for that new life and adventure.

Chapter 3
New Friends

Some days out on the trail, Brad had camped for the night near a small stream. He built a small fire to keep him warm and cook a rabbit he had shot earlier. He had just finished off the rabbit and was about to settle in for a good night's rest when he heard the gunfire. He quickly put out the camp fire, grabbing his gun along with the supplies. Off he ran in the direction the shot came from, about a quarter of a mile downstream from his location.

Through the trees he saw a campfire with a wagon. There, near the fire, he saw a man and woman older than he. Brad yelled out.

"Hey there in the camp. Is everything all right?"

He could see the man grab his gun after he started to shout.

"I mean you know harm."

Brad walked out from the trees with his gun in one hand raised high.

"I heard a shot, from my camp just up river. I was thinking someone might be in trouble down here."

"If everything is alright here, I'll just go back."

After some coaxing from his wife the man spoke up.

"Hold up there, young man."

"My wife and I would like to thank you for your concern, but it was only a snake that crawled into our camp and scared my wife."

"Would you like to stay and share some of our meal?"

"We would really enjoy some of your conversation."

"Sure. I've already eaten, but that stew smells good, and I would surely enjoy some conversation too. It been a long time since I've talked to anybody but myself."

After a hot bowl of stew, he found out the young couple were heading to St. Louis. He informed them he was heading that way, but he was looking to end up out west in the mountains. Upon hearing this they invited Brad to go along to St. Louis. Brad said he would enjoy their company as they told him they would enjoy his. They spent most of the night getting aquatinted.

Brad was glad he was along, it meant a little added protection along the trail to St. Louis for all of them. Brad would hunt for the nightly meal and sleep under the wagon only when it rained. Their journey together went without any incidents from that point on.

A week had gone by and they were getting close. His eyes lit up when he saw the mighty Mississippi River. They turned south heading for St. Louis, when they came across the camp of a mountain man. His name was Jim Beaver. Half white, half Pawnee Indian, but in Brad's eye all mountain man. At night they listen to Jim's stories of mountain living, and the stories of hunting and trapping beaver. Brad knew this was the life he wanted to live. Before long Brad asked Jim if he would take him along to the mountains and teach him how to be a mountain man.

Jim thought it over, asked Brad a few questions, and received the right answers. He reckon he needed a partner. His last one died of the fever last winter. Being informed that Jim would teach him, Brad was even more excited about going to the mountains. They would leave and go into St. Louis for supplies next morning before heading west. Before they retired for the evening Brad needed to tell Jim about his past. After revealing his past, Brad told Jim he knew all Indians weren't bad. Jim smiled at Brad and said.

"Remember only half of me is Indian so that makes me only half bad, only my white half."

All laughed before settling down for a night of rest.

Chapter 4
Heading West

Upon reaching St. Louis Brad and his traveling friends parted ways as they were going to stay in Missouri. Jim knew Brad had no money, so he offered Brad a grubstake of a horse, a new long gun, and supplies for the long journey. Brad promised to repay him out of the money he would get from his half of the pelts at the next summer rendezvous. Packed and ready, they headed west leaving civilization. Jim told Brad he was going to love eating prairie chickens.

"What's a prairie chicken?" asked Brad.

It was a long hard ride, especially leading two pack horses full of supplies. With luck it would take a little over four weeks to reach Jim's cabin in the Rockies. Along the way at night, they ate prairie chicken, and Jim told brad all about the Indians, buffalo and wildlife they may come across, things Brad had only heard stories about.

Days out, while stopping to make camp, Brad thought how lucky he had been. They had just settled in for sleep. Brad arose when he heard the sound of an animal in the far-off distance. He quickly grabbed for his gun before Jim informed him it was just the yip of a coyote.

"Maybe I should teach you the difference between coyote and Indian, but soon you will learn." said Jim lying back down to get some rest.

There would be plenty Brad would need to know if he was to survive. Brad was a fast learner as Jim would come to find out.

Jim gave Brad a knife and showed him how to throw and use it. Brad got really good at handling it, and in a short time Brad was deadly accurate throwing it. Jim also found out how good a shot his new partner was. Something Jim admired and came to appreciate later on.

It was just two weeks into their trek when Jim told Brad he wanted to stop and see his mother and rest some before they continued their journey. Brad told Jim he was looking forward to seeing a town. Jim couldn't help but laugh. Brad wondered what was so funny.

Chapter 5
The Visit and Visitors

It wasn't long before he found out while they were approaching a Pawnee Indian village with an escort that seemed to come from everywhere. They rode together with their Pawnee escort right up to his mother's teepee. They spent two days resting themselves and the horses. Brad heard the story of how Jim's white mother was captured by the Crow Indians and traded to the Pawnee. She became the wife of a great warrior and together they had Jim.

His Pawnee father wanted to call him White Beaver. His mother wanted to call him Jim, after her father, hence the name Jim Beaver. His mother made sure she taught him white man's English. This helped the tribe when settlers began heading west. Jim never felt he truly belonged and reaching age seventeen he left the tribe for good. He then met his partner who taught him how to be a mountain man. Together they were a pretty good team as Jim taught him Indian sign and tongue, just as Jim is now teaching Brad.

It came time came to leave the village. Jim said his last goodbye to his mother. His father had been killed some time back by another raiding tribe. His mother, on account of her hard years, looked old and frail. Maybe she wouldn't last through the winter.

Jim was very sad leaving his mother as she was very much an Indian now. He wanted to take her along, but she wanted to die as an Indian from her village. A tear ran down Jim's cheek as he and Brad again rode the trail west knowing he may never see his mother again. Brad understood and knew this feeling as he waved goodbye to her.

Three days out from the tribe, while Brad was sleeping, Jim covered Brads mouth. Not letting Brad make a sound, he needed to wake him from his sleep. Using his hand, he signed to Brad there were Indians around. Jim had already put out the fire when he heard their Indian wildlife calls. In the dark they sat there with guns ready. A war cry, then another, as the Blackfeet warriors ran out from the brush. Two shots rang out as both Jim and Brad dropped the warrior's dead in their tracks. Another war cry shrieked out from just over Brad's shoulder. He turned while pulling his knife and catching the warrior. Wrestling the brave to the ground, after a short struggle, Brad planted his knife deep within the warrior's chest. The warrior had succumbed to death by the hands of Brad and his knife.

Both men scrambled back together, back to back, waiting for more attacks that never came. It was over as they heard one horse ride away. Brad was ever so glad Jim was alert standing guard. From that moment on Brad became a light sleeper. Quickly they packed up and left the camp hoping no more Indians were coming through the area. They weren't.

Chapter 6
Bear Encounter

Brad now got to see his first Buffalo herd. Tanaka Jim called them, as far as one man could see grazing across the prairie. This reminded Brad of the stories of herds so large it took the better part of the day to pass by. Brad saw a mountain lion feeding on an elk carcass protecting it from a hungry coyote, these things opened Brad's eyes to the west.

Jim told Brad that any day now they would get their first look at the Rocky Mountains. Then the day finally came. Brad saw them and with each day that passed, they got closer to the mountains until they reached the foothills. In a few days they would arrive in the valley and the cabin Jim and his former partner had built.

Then, just a day from Brad's cabin, something happened Jim or Brad would never forget. Jim was leading about twenty yards ahead when Brad saw Jim's horse rise on his hind legs. Jim fell off the back as his horse galloped off. Something spooked the horse, but Brad wasn't able to see it. Brad rode up with the pack horses in tow and asked Jim if he was alright. Jim nodded that he was fine.

"What spooked the horse Jim?"

"Darn if I know what spooked him, maybe a snake."

Brad left the pack horses with Jim and he took off after Jim's horse.

Jim let the pack horses graze. Then he climbed upon a boulder just in case there was a snake nearby. His sense of smell picked up a foul odor blowing toward him. Something smelled dead and he looked around to see if he could see it. At the same time the pack horses also picked up the scent and bolted off quickly. Jim, knew he should have held onto those horses. He wouldn't let this happen again as long as he lived.

He looked around and not more than fifteen feet away was the carcass of a dead deer. The kill was fresh. Too fresh! Something this fresh could only mean one thing. Whatever killed it was still in the area. Now Jim began to worry. Looking around, fear raced through his body. There, about fifty or sixty yards away was a big grizzly heading his way.

Jim had but only one plan and it wasn't the greatest. He ran. Fast as he could toward the direction Brad had ridden off. He only wished he had his gun that was still with his horse. His only hope was a stand of thick trees he thought would slow up the bear.

Jim was fast but not as fast as the grizzly. The little distance he had for a head start was shrinking fast when he reached the tree line. It slowed the bear alright, but it also slowed Jim.

He was able to keep a slim fifteen yard lead when he saw Brad coming his way with horses in tow.

"BEAR! BEAR! SHOOT HIM!" shouted Jim.

Brad pulled up upon hearing Jim's warning. Quickly Brad dropped all the reins of the horses and readied his gun as Jim was departing the trees with a grizzly hot on his tail.

Still mounted on his horse, Brad took steady aim and pulled the trigger from about twenty yards away. Jim's eyes got even bigger as he felt the slug pass near his head and then he heard the bear roar. It was a direct hit that caused the bear to stumble down for just a bit. Jim ran past Brad and straight to his horse grabbing for his gun.

The bear was down but not for long as he rose to his hind legs. Letting out a blood curling roar before he started his next charge. Brad was still loading another round when he hear a shot from behind him and saw the bear fall. The attack was over, but Brad put another slug into the grizzly just to be sure.

That night Jim showed Brad how to skin the bear of his hide. Bear steaks were going to be the main course for their nightly meal. After the meal and checking on the horses, both men sat around the fire warming up. Jim spoke up after Brad had a chance to settle in with a hot cup of coffee.

"Say Brad, that shot you took at the grizzly was close to my head."

"So, it needed to be taken." said Brad.

"Brad I would like to know, what was you thinking?"

"Me, I was thinking if I missed the bear, maybe I would get you and I'd be able to get away."

He smiled at Jim.

"You're too good a shot for that to happen, Right!"

"Well, I was shaking a lot." said Brad.

"What a darn partner your turning out to be." as he threw his empty cup at Brad.

"You better hope I don't lift your scalp while you sleep as I got first watch."

Jim said this as he was sharpening his knife.

Brad just pulled his blanket up around him saying. "Wake me in a few partner."

Jim shook his head and smiled.

Next day as they started to ride away, Jim pointed out to Brad the way to the cabin and let him take the lead. Jim let his gun rest across his lap while chewing on leftover bear steak. He rode along with the bear hide rolled up behind him leading the pack horses. From this day forward both men would come to rely on each other a lot.

Chapter 7
Mountain Life

They finally arrived at the cabin. It was situated on the edge of the forest and backed up against a rock wall on three sides to provide some safety and protection from the wind. It was just a short ride from the cabin by horse to a small river filled with fish, beaver and muskrat. There was a beautiful valley that was a feeding meadow for elk and other game like bears and mountain lions looking for a meal.

Jim taught Brad how to trap and tan hides. The winds of winter came over time and would blow. The snow piled up but this never stopped their activities. There was never a shortage of fresh game for trapping or food. Jim taught Brad a lot that first year. Throughout their many years together they could almost tell what the other was thinking. By the end of that first year Brad could speak the Indian tongue and sign as good as Jim.

Each year, summer after summer, they would travel to the great rendezvous, looking to trade their pelts for supplies to last out another long winter; mostly for shot, traps, whiskey and anything else they would need. They saw many of their old friends and made new ones. Brad once won a new long rifle, then a horse, in a yearly shooting competition. Knife throwing won him and Jim brand new knives. They both became well known to all the other mountain men and Indians. Jim even saw some braves from his tribe and got in a good match of Indian leg wrestling. Then, the time would always come to say goodbye for another year. They hoped all would return but some did not.

Brad and Jim could read tracks better than most. They knew the mountains and every trail up into them. They helped a wagon train track down a band of renegade Indians who kidnaped some of their women. Even the Army used their special talents to hunt and guide supply wagons from one fort to another. Trapping was their livelihood and living in the mountains was all they needed, only traveling to a local settlement once in a while for the company of a woman.

You never saw one of them turn down a good brisk drink or fail to join in a battle of fist. They could lie, spit further, or drink more than any other man alive. No man or beast would ever come between them. The friendly Indian tribes came to respect each man. The bad came to fear them.

Chapter 8
Snake Bite

One day upon returning from another rendezvous and trading furs, they were leaving Wyoming and going to their cabin in the mountains. Brad's life was about to hang in the balance. The day was very hot, and they decided to call it a day early when they reached the Green River. They were hot and dripping with sweat, and they couldn't wait to take a swim to cool off and get some trail dust washed from their clothes.

Brad dismounted, taking care of the horses before he would walk down to the river. Jim, like always, was in charge of getting the fire going after gathering some dry wood. Brad was done with the horse and walked down to the river's edge. Then, Brad heard the familiar sound of a rattler. Jim heard it also. Before Brad could locate it, he was struck just above the right ankle.

Jim, upon hearing the rattler picked up his gun just as Brad was bitten. Running toward Brad Jim stopped and blew the head of the snake clean off. Dropping the gun, he grabbed his knife from within his boot and attended to Brad.

Cutting and ripping at Brad's right pant leg he saw the two puncture wounds. It was time to react as he told Brad to lay quiet and try not to move. With his knife he cut across the bite and allowed the blood to flow out before he started to suck out the poison. In short time Jim gripped Brad across his shoulders and pulled and carried him back to the fire.

Jim being part Indian remembered his tribe's medicine man would fix a bag of herbs and mud to draw poison from the wounds. All these years he carried a small bag of these herbs in his pack. It was time to use it. He went back to his pack and took the bag out and headed back toward the river.

At the river Jim scooped up a handful of mud, placed it on a rock, then he mixed in some herbs. Taking his neck scarf, he placed the mud mixture in it and took it back to Brad. Looking at Brad's leg he could now see it was swelling. He placed the mud mixture on the bite and tied the scarf tightly around his leg to keep it there. Then he grabbed a blanket and draped it over Brad.

The fire was going well when Jim looked over at Brad and saw the chills were now setting in. He grabbed Brad's blanket and spread it out also over Brad. All he could do now was to lay cold cloths of river water across his forehead and wipe the cool water around his face. When the chills set in, he kept him warm and waited.

Jim knew it would be touch-and-go throughout the night as he replaced his remedy every hour and kept up the cold-water cloths. Finally, Brad stopped shivering and dropped off to sleep. Jim continued to care for him before he himself dropped off from exhaustion. It was just an hour before dawn.

Jim didn't hear the two Shoshone Indians ride into camp. They saw the mud treatment on Brad's leg and began to care for him as Jim slept. When Jim awoke, he saw the braves. He quickly got to his feet, but knew they were friendly, before seeing Brad sitting up eating some snake meat the Indian's had cooked up.

Jim was glad to see Brad had pulled through. One brave held up the snake rattle and skin for both of them to see. The brave then signed for Jim to eat snake also. Jim nodded and took a big piece smiling at Brad. Brad thanked them all and took another bite of snake. Jim then held up the bag of herbs and told Brad how he prepared it in case he had to use it on him. Brad suggested they needed to get more first chance. Jim agreed, and he took another piece of snake.

"Sort of taste like prairie chicken you think?"

Brad, the two Indians, and Jim stayed two days until Brad was able to ride. The Indians would hunt, Jim kept an eye out for snakes and wild animals, while Brad slept getting his strength back. The day came to move on as Jim and Brad thanked the warriors with gifts of extra knives, they had. They all helped Brad on his horse before they themselves mounted theirs. They all signed in Indian, a sign which referred to safe journey, then they rode off. Jim looked at Brad before turning his horse leading Brad and pack horses toward their cabin in the mountains.

Chapter 9
Losing A Friend

Stories were told about how they fought off hundreds of hostile Indians and even took down a grizzly with nothing but knives. Stories, true or not, are the things that make men legends. Jim and Brad never said they weren't tall tales. So, these stories stuck along with many others and they grew.

Brad spent year after year hunting and trapping with his good friend Jim Beaver. Brad was looking and living all the part of a mountain man. He was living his dream. Jim had taught Brad well, feeling he was at least his equal, maybe even just a touch better.

Jim was more than ten years older than Brad. Jim being in his late sixties. He could stay up with Brad for the most part, but Father Time was catching up on old Jim. It took a little longer to get moving and longer rides were taking a big toll.

Feeling his age, Jim wanted to stay and work on some small projects around the cabin. The day before had been a long ride for the both of them as they rode to a local settlement and back for the supplies they needed badly. Brad decided he would go hunting for game to build up their meat storage. Maybe his old friend would get some rest if needed. Jim agreed.

After a short rest, Jim went out to gather wood and grass to repair a leaky roof. I guess Jim relied too much on Brad to watch his back. He forgot Brad was not around this time and caution was thrown to the wind. He didn't notice something was hidden far back in the tall grass. Little warning was given as a mighty mountain lion sprung upon him. Jim had no chance. Jim Beaver paid with his life.

Brad returned to find what was left of his good friend then he buried him not far behind their cabin. He made a cross, and said a word for his soul, spending the rest of the day there at Jim's grave. He recalled their days and adventures together and tears began to flow. He blamed himself for not staying.

More than eight years had passed, and he missed his good friend. He continued to spend the summers and winters high up in his mountain paradise. Still trapping and hunting the wildlife. Now in his late sixties, Brad had seen the expansion of the West and wanted nothing to do with civilization. Life in the mountains suited him just fine.

He knew his time on earth was running out, but he didn't dwell on it much. He did what he could. Winter would be here any day now and lots needed to be done.

Chapter 10
Remembering

Brad once found an orphaned wolf pup and he raised him to keep him company. He called him Wolf, and they trapped and hunted together, forming a strong wonderful bond.

Brad woke up to the first light snow of the season in the mountains. He felt cold as he put a couple of logs on the fire. The cabin was warming up just fine and he drank some coffee while he and Wolf ate. The cold, along with his old age, wouldn't allow his old bones to move as they used too. Sitting there, his mind wondered back, remembering for the first time in so many years his family.

He could see his mother and father clearly in his mind. The old cabin and of course him playing with his sister Jenny. How his life took such a huge turn as the Indians killed Morgan and Molly Smith along with his sister Jenny; him being a young man setting out for the West. The older couple, darn if he couldn't remember their names, allowing him to travel along to St. Louis. Then there was the trek west with Jim Beaver, and his life as a mountain man. He thought it was funny how these things just suddenly came to him after all these years.

"Can't sit here all day, Wolf. Time to check those traps before the snow comes down to heavy and I won't be able to see."

He didn't need to clean up. There was plenty of time for that when he returned. He sat there just a little longer looking around the old cabin when he thought he heard Jim calling to him.

"Let's get going old timer."

"Fine, just don't be in no big hurry." replied Brad. He looked around seeing only Wolf who was tilting his head in puzzlement.

"Wolf, I must be losing my mind. Why of course I am. I am talking to you."

It was in his mind alright, but it sounded so real.

"Okay Wolf, Let's get going."

Putting on his heavy coat, hat, mittens and grabbing his old gun, he headed for the door. He paused and turned back, putting a couple more of the big logs on the fire.

"Wolf this is going to keep this old cabin nice and warm upon our return."

At the door he stopped to look back again. Wanting to see the inside of the cabin he and Jim shared together all these years. Turning while opening the door, he faced the cold outside. Through the door both he and Wolf went.

He pulled the door closed as he had done all these numerous times. Amazed as he watched the snow fall up the valley along the river. He put his tongue out to catch some snowflakes.

He knew not why, but he and Wolf turned to the side of the cabin and walked to the back toward Jim's grave.

He took off his mittens, then kneeled, laying a hand on Jim's grave as he spoke.

"Dear old friend, another winter has come. I wonder how many more before I come to join you again."

He stood up and put his mittens back on. Then he walked away toward his horse, for a ride in the snow into his beloved valley.

Epilogue

For the last few years friendly Indians would stop by to visit and trade with Jim and Brad. After Jim's death they still came around, once in the spring, also in the summer and again in the late fall, checking up on old Brad. Brad really enjoyed their company. It gave him the chance to brush up on Indian sign and tongue. They brought him meat, and then one other time his heavy buffalo coat. Brad would go hunting with them and share stories of his and Jim's many adventures.

The next day after Brad departed the cabin it was a very cold night, with snow on the ground. Indians came around to check on Brad and found him frozen. He died of an apparent heart attack near one of his traps. Wolf was lying there next to him still alive. They buried Brad alongside his best friend Jim, doing what Brad had told them he wished many times. They lay together in the mountains they both loved. Wolf stayed until they finished then ran away into the valley.

Before leaving the valley, the Indians burned the cabin down. Returning the land to nature as both men would have wanted. Riding away, they paused on a hill after hearing a lone wolf howl. Hearing his sorrow-song down in the valley, and sitting astride their ponies, they remembered for the last time their friends, Jim Beaver and Brad Johnson. These men, who were the legend of true mountain men.

About the Author

Harry Everly was born 24 February 1950 in Zanesville, Ohio, and was raised near New Concord, Ohio, the boyhood home of the astronaut John Glenn. He attended school at Perry Elementary, and New Concord Junior High before graduating from John Glenn High School, class of 1968. He enlisted in the Air Force retiring after 24 years. He's a veteran of the Vietnam and Persian Gulf wars. Harry  had the honor of being selected to the maintenance team for the United States Air Force Demonstration Team, "The Thunderbirds." He lives today in Colorado Springs, CO, with his dog Cactus. His hobbies include travel, taking landscape and wildlife photography, and writing. He enjoys his Air Force Falcons, the Ohio State Buckeyes, and the Cleveland Indians…longsuffering Browns fan….

Harry Everly Story Collections

Grizzly Impact: Terror Comes in All Forms, None Worse than A Grizzly

Harry Everly Stories: Volume-1
Three Short Stories

- Montana Lane
- The Legend of King Grizzly's Hunt
- Terror in Montana Territory

Montana Lane

Montana Lane was a cow puncher who rode the fence up in the high country for the Twin River Ranch. Along with his partner Ted, they had plans 'till the day came when their whole world changed—when a grizzly claimed the mountain.

The Legend of King Grizzlies Hunt

The stories mountain men tell are many. None more than a legend of a grizzly bear called King Grizzly, Bobcat Bob hunts down this grizzly with

his Indian blood brother Running Deer to revenge
the death of their good friend Whiskey Bill.

Terror in the Montana Territory
    Montana was a wild and formidable place
in 1875. Terror was in the form of a monster
grizzly that came down from Canada. All who
live in this part of the territory and on the Cross
Bow Ranch needed to survive this intruder or
die trying.

Myths and Legends of the Mountains: Myths and Legends Come in All Forms, Some Are Even Animals

Harry Everly Stories: Volume-2
Four Short Stories

- Night of the Wolves
- Monarch of the Pass
- Roar of the Mountain
- Legend of True Mountain Men

Myths and Legends of the Mountains is a four-short-story novel, about men, two animals, and a creature that lives among them.

Night of the Wolves
Rudyard Kipling said, "The strength of the pack is the wolf, and the strength of the wolf is the pack." Could it be more than this, maybe even human, for one wolf named Blue Eyes?

Monarch of the Pass
Not all legends are about men or their deeds.
Monarch was not your typical young elk. His life
growing up changed as he now needed to avoid
one Indian who crossed his path more than once.
Maybe the great spirit would intervene?

Roar of the Mountain
They said the Indians knew of this mountain
creature, but few had ever seen what made the
mighty roar. The curiosity of a mountain man,
with the aid of two Indian braves, led him to hunt
down whatever it was, even if his horse had a
different opinion.

Legend of True Mountain Men
Some say it took a special breed to be a mountain
man. A life of freedom, but no less a hard life
for one so young. A boy, becoming a man, who
wanted this way of life, then setting out to achieve
it. With the help of a half-breed Indian, who
became his mentor and friend, he lived the life he
chose.

Coming Soon

Friends and Heroes: A Friend Can Be A Hero, A Hero Can Be A Friend

Harry Everly Stories: Volume-3
Four Short Stories

- Legend of Jasper Dallas
- A New Beginning, A New Life
- Johnny Blue-Coat
- Being A Soldier

www.ingramcontent.com/pod-product-compliance
Lightning Source LLC
Chambersburg PA
CBHW071502030726
47593CB00003B/1118